Cold Whispers II

# FRIGHT at the FREEMONT LIBRARY

by Dee Phillips

illustrated by Tom Connell

BEARPORT PUBLISHING

New York, New York

**Credits**

Cover, © photogl/Shutterstock, © Marko Bradic/Shutterstock, © spinetta/Shutterstock, and © Africa Studio/Shutterstock.

Publisher: Kenn Goin
Editor: Jessica Rudolph
Creative Director: Spencer Brinker

Library of Congress Cataloging-in-Publication Data in process at time of publication (2017)
Library of Congress Control Number: 2016020329
ISBN-13: 978-1-944102-36-4 (library binding)

For more information, write to Bearport Publishing Company, Inc., 45 West 21st Street, Suite 3B, New York, New York 10010.
Printed in the United States of America.

10 9 8 7 6 5 4 3 2 1

# Contents

# CHAPTER 1

# A Visit to the Library

It was a cool spring afternoon as Jane turned her wheelchair onto Main Street and made her way toward the Abraham Freemont Library.

Jane was spending her vacation with her aunt, who worked as a librarian. Aunt Beth had told her niece all about the library's extraordinary collection of old books, and Jane couldn't wait to see them for herself.

When Jane reached the library, she looked up at the big windows and gray stone walls. Thick green ivy clung to the stonework and danced in the chilly breeze. More than one hundred years ago, the building had been the home of a wealthy family. Now only the first floor was in use and the upper floors were closed off.

Jane wheeled up the ramp to enter the library. Aunt Beth peered around a huge stack of books on the checkout counter and gave Jane a big grin.

"Hi, honey," she said. "What have you been up to all day?"

"I've been in the park, reading," answered Jane, smiling.

"Of course! Why did I even ask?" laughed her aunt.

For as long as Jane could remember, she'd loved to read and write. She even wrote for her school paper and dreamed of becoming a prize-winning **journalist**. She was always on the lookout for an interesting story to write about.

"Take a look around, Jane," said Aunt Beth. "The library will be open for another hour."

Jane took in her surroundings. Close to the checkout counter were comfortable sofas, shelves with the latest bestsellers, and desks where visitors could use the library's computers.

She moved toward the rear of the building and entered the huge Freemont Collection Room, where the **rare** books were

kept. Few visitors came to this room, and Jane found herself all alone among shelves of dusty books and silvery spiderwebs. The bookshelves towered up to the ceiling, separated by shadowy passageways. The warm air smelled of wood, leather, and old paper.

Hanging at the end of one set of bookshelves was a photograph of an elderly man. Below the photo's brass frame was a small **plaque**.

*Abraham Freemont*
*(1840–1925)*

*Businessman Abraham Freemont lived in Appleton his entire life. After his death, he left his vast fortune, home, and book collection to the town. It is thanks to his generosity that this library and Freemont Park exist today.*

Jane peered at the old man in the picture. She thought she could detect a **menacing** glint in his eyes. *But he must've been a wonderful man,* Jane reasoned. *Without him, this amazing library wouldn't be here.*

Jane **maneuvered** her wheelchair between two sets of shelves and reached for a book about wildflowers from 1903. Its crumbling cover was made of pale blue leather. Inside the book was an **inscription** to a girl named Emma:

*For our Dearest Emma,*
*Happy Birthday!*
*With Love, Mama and Papa*
*September 30, 1903*

As Jane carefully turned the **fragile** pages, she suddenly got the feeling that someone was watching her. She twisted her head to look around, but the aisle was empty.

Jane placed the wildflower book back on the shelf. Then, from the next aisle, she heard the sound of someone turning the pages of a book. She moved to the end of the aisle and peered into the shadows. The library's dim lighting made it difficult to see.

"Hello?" she said. But the only sound Jane heard was the creaking of the wooden floorboards under her wheels as she moved slowly down the aisle.

Suddenly, the air around Jane turned icy cold. It was so cold, she felt as if she'd climbed into a refrigerator. *Did someone just turn on the air conditioner at full blast?* she thought.

Shivering, Jane looked at the shelves to her left and right. The feeling of being watched was now even more powerful. The hairs on the back of her neck rose. Then, out of nowhere . . .

*Whoosh . . . Thud!*

A book flew off one of the shelves and fell on the floor directly in front of her.

With her heart thumping in her chest, Jane leaned forward to look at the book.

## JANE EYRE
### by Charlotte Brontë

It was the book Jane's parents had named her after! Jane twisted and turned to look in every direction. Was someone playing a joke on her?

Then Jane heard the sound of heels clicking on the wooden floors. Aunt Beth appeared at the end of the aisle. "Jane, is everything okay? I heard a loud noise." She looked down and stooped to pick up *Jane Eyre*.

"I . . . I . . . don't know," said Jane, feeling a little shaken. "This book fell right off the shelf."

"Don't worry, honey," said Aunt Beth. "Some of these old bookshelves are very rickety."

Aunt Beth placed the book back on the shelf and then gave Jane's hand a reassuring squeeze. "Jane, you're absolutely frozen!" she exclaimed. "That's strange. It feels pretty warm in here to me."

Jane realized her aunt was right. Suddenly, the ice-cold air was now warmer.

"Come on," said Aunt Beth. "Let's get you home and warmed up." She hurried off ahead of Jane, straightening books as she walked. "We'll pick up pizza on the way. How does that sound?"

When her aunt mentioned supper, Jane realized how hungry she was.

"Yeah, pizza sounds good," Jane replied.

As Jane followed her aunt, she noticed that the shelves in the library *were* rickety. *Maybe that's what caused the book to fall,* she thought. *And parts of the old building are **drafty**. I probably should have worn a thicker sweater.*

Jane and her aunt reached the entrance of the Freemont Collection Room, and Aunt Beth began to turn off the room's lights, aisle by aisle. Jane turned and looked back. Between the tall shelves of books, she was sure she could see something moving in the moonlight. A soft, gray shape—almost like a wispy cloud—seemed to be hovering in and out of the shadows.

Then, as Aunt Beth switched off the last light, the bookshelves were **plunged** into darkness.

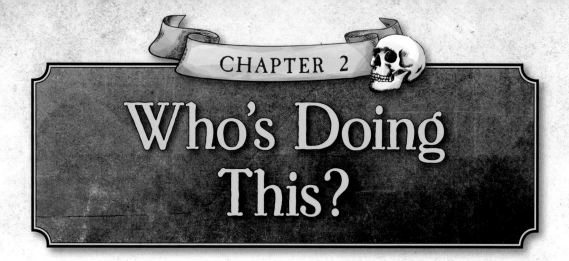

# CHAPTER 2

# Who's Doing This?

The next morning, Jane still felt uneasy about what had happened the previous day. Still, she had been looking forward to reading some of the old books in the library, so she decided to go to work with her aunt.

Jane spent the day reading, and by late afternoon, most of the visitors to the library were gone. She was alone again in the Freemont Collection Room. She was **engrossed** in the diary of a nineteenth-century explorer when she heard something.

*Tap. Tap. Tap. Tap.*

Jane closed her book and slowly moved around the bookshelves toward the sound. There, in a dark corner, stood an old wooden desk with an **antique** typewriter on it.

*Tap. Tap. Tap. Tap.*

As Jane moved toward the tapping sound, the air around her became **frigid** and her breath formed a small white cloud. She wheeled closer to the desk. To her shock, the typewriter keys were moving on their own!

Jane watched as four of the keys moved down and up, one after the other, over and over.

*Tap* J . . . *Tap* A . . . *Tap* N . . . *Tap* E . . .

Jane noticed that the four letters spelled out her name. "Who's doing this?" she said into the icy air. "Who's typing my name? What are you trying to tell me?"

As if to answer her question, the typing stopped, and Jane heard a loud thud in one of the aisles behind her. She followed the sound. Lying on the floor was the book, *Jane Eyre*.

Then two more books were hurled to the floor—*Bang! Thud!* Jane was stunned.

*Bang!* Another book crashed to the floor.

Then several more books landed in front of her.

Aunt Beth heard the racket and rushed to the aisle.

"Are you okay, honey?" asked Aunt Beth.

"They just kept flying off the shelves," Jane cried out. She pointed to the ground. "And look! They're all lined up in a row face up!"

Aunt Beth looked at the books lying in the aisle. "How odd," she said worriedly. "I'll get someone to fix these old shelves. Don't worry, I'll put the books back."

"Wait!" Jane said.

Jane took her cell phone out of her book bag and snapped a picture. Then, as Aunt Beth reshelved each of the books, Jane looked at the picture on her phone. Could someone—or something—in the library be trying to make contact with her?

Jane was determined to get to the bottom of the mystery.

# CHAPTER 3

# The Message

Late that evening, Jane lay in bed, unable to get warm. She held her cell phone and stared at the picture of the books. Why were they all lined up in a row?

Finally, Jane sat up and grabbed a notebook and pen on her bedside table. She hurriedly wrote out the names of the books in the order they'd fallen to the floor. Could there be a message in the titles?

A thought occurred to Jane. She focused on the first words in each title and circled them.

JANE EYRE

THE PRISONER OF ZENDA

CRIME AND PUNISHMENT

BLACK BEAUTY

SECRETS OF CONJURING AND MAGIC

THROUGH THE LOOKING GLASS

THE TIME MACHINE

EMMA

Jane wrote out the phrase formed by the words she had circled.

*Jane, prisoner crime black secrets through*
*time . . . Emma*

What could the message mean? Was Emma the girl who'd received the book about wildflowers for her birthday in 1903? Had she been a prisoner? What crime had taken place?

That night, Jane barely slept. She couldn't stop thinking about the message. She needed to figure out what was going on. And that meant returning to the library and digging around.

Jane spent the next day at the library. Just before closing time, she told Aunt Beth she was going to the bookstore down the street, and she would call her aunt later. Instead of leaving the library, however, Jane snuck off and hid in the storage room. She wanted to explore the library while it was empty, but she knew her aunt wouldn't approve.

The cramped storage room was stacked with boxes and old furniture. In the gloomy light, she noticed two small beady

eyes peering at her. Jane's heart nearly jumped out of her chest, but to her relief, she realized she was looking into a dusty glass case containing a **taxidermy** animal.

Jane took a deep breath and waited. Soon, the narrow strip of bright light beneath the storage room door went dark as her aunt switched off all the lights and left the building. Now Jane was alone in the library.

She opened the door and moved into the eerie darkness. The only sounds she could hear were her own breathing and the gentle whirr of her wheels.

She headed toward the Freemont Collection Room.

"Hello?" she called out, feeling afraid. "Is anyone there?"

Slowly, Jane moved between the shelves, in and out of the faint moonlight. At any moment, she expected the air to turn icy cold or to see a book fly from the shelves.

Then, suddenly, Jane *knew* she was being watched. She nervously turned a full circle and saw it . . . a small movement. The same wispy cloud she'd seen before was floating toward the desk in the far corner.

Jane held her breath. She knew what was coming next.

*Tap. Tap. Tap. Tap.*

## CHAPTER 4

# Emma's Story

As Jane moved toward the desk, the terrible frigid air she'd felt before **penetrated** her bones. She watched as the typewriter keys slowly tapped out the letters of her name.

Then other keys began to move very fast. Someone was trying to send a message to her. But the keys were moving so quickly that Jane couldn't follow what words were being formed.

"Hold on!" she cried. "I can't understand. You're going too fast."

Jane pulled her laptop from her bag and opened it on the desk. "Here," she called out into the air. "Can you write a message on my laptop? Like this."

She typed the word JANE, then waited. Within seconds, the laptop keys began to tap by themselves, and words appeared on the screen: *Will you help me?*

"Yes, I'll help you," said Jane softly.

A message slowly began to **emerge** on the screen:

JANE

Will you help me?

I'm Emma Freemont. This library was once my home. My parents died in an accident when I was 12 years old. My uncle, Abraham Freemont, became my **guardian**. He was to care for me until I was 18, when I would **inherit** my family's fortune. As my 18th birthday drew near, my uncle locked me in the attic. He wanted to inherit my fortune himself.

So he left me to die with no food or water.

An awful feeling swept over Jane. She remembered thinking that Emma's uncle had a menacing look in his eyes.

"What can I do, Emma?" she whispered into the darkness.

After a few moments, more words appeared on the screen:

I want everyone to know the truth about what happened to me. Then I might be set free from my home.

Jane desperately wanted to help, but who would ever believe this incredible story? Was there even any proof?

The laptop screen flickered:

This desk was once in the attic where I was kept prisoner. Feel beneath the desk and you will find a silk ribbon.

Jane carefully ran her fingers under the wooden desk. Then, in a section where two pieces of wood were joined, her fingers felt something soft and silky. It was a ribbon, just as Emma had described.

"I found it!" gasped Jane. "What should I do now?"

Pull on the ribbon.

Jane did as instructed, and a shallow drawer popped out from the side of the desk. Inside the secret drawer was a small, leather-bound diary.

Jane gently lifted the diary from the drawer and opened it. The daily entries described visits to church, walks in the countryside, and thoughts about the books Emma had been reading. As Jane turned the pages, however, the story of Emma's tragic final days unfolded.

*September 20, 1909*

*I am very concerned about my uncle's cruel behavior. He forbids me to leave the house. Today, I heard him tell one of the servants that I am very ill and she should not come near me. But I am not sick!*

Jane slowly turned the yellowed pages.

*September 25, 1909*

*My uncle has locked me in the tiny attic room with no food or water. He has put iron bars across the window. I keep calling for help, but no one comes. I believe he may have sent the servants away.*

*September 28, 1909*

*It has been days, and still my uncle ignores my cries. I am so weak from hunger, and my throat burns for a sip of water.*

Jane hung her head and a tear rolled down her cheek. What a horrifying end for young Emma! It was much too late to save the girl, but the terrible story laid out in her diary would prove what had happened in the old library.

"I'll tell your story, Emma," said Jane as she closed the diary. "I'll find a way to let everyone know what your uncle did."

Jane looked at the screen of her laptop. Three final words appeared:

Thank you, Jane.

As she stared at the last message, Jane realized the air around her was growing warmer. She closed the secret drawer in the desk and carefully placed her laptop and Emma's diary in her book bag.

Jane made her way to the library's front entrance, unlocked the door, and wheeled out of the building. She wondered what the best way to help Emma would be. Then Jane formed an idea. She would write a story for the local newspaper, and everyone would know the true history of the old library. Abraham Freemont was a celebrated figure in the town. The **revelation** that he was a murderer would be shocking news.

Already, the words to tell Emma's story were forming in Jane's mind. Hopefully, when the story was finally told, Emma's **spirit** could find peace.

Jane pulled her cell phone from her bag and dialed Aunt Beth's number. She had a lot to explain.

"Aunt Beth," Jane said, "I think I have an idea for a news story. . . . One that will make a difference."

# Fright at the Freemont Library

1. What is happening in this scene?

2. Why do you think Emma's ghost chose Jane to uncover the secret of her death? Use examples from the story to explain your thoughts.

3. Write Emma's diary entry for September 26, 1909. What do you think she's feeling?

4. Why do you think Abraham Freemont left the fortune he stole from his niece, Emma, to the town of Appleton?

5. Send a secret message to a friend using the first word of book titles. What books from your school library would you use to create the message?

# GLOSSARY

**antique** (an-TEEK) an object that is valuable because of its age

**drafty** (DRAF-tee) having cold air moving through in a way that is uncomfortable

**emerge** (ih-MURJ) to come out from somewhere hidden

**engrossed** (en-GROHSD) having all of one's attention or interest absorbed by something

**fragile** (FRAJ-uhl) easily broken or damaged

**frigid** (FRIJ-ihd) extremely cold

**guardian** (GAHR-dee-uhn) someone who takes care of a person

**inherit** (in-HERR-uht) to receive something, such as money, from someone who has died

**inscription** (in-SKRIP-shuhn) words that have been carved or written onto a surface

**journalist** (JUR-nuh-list) someone who collects information and writes articles

**maneuvered** (muh-NOO-vurd) moved in a careful way

**menacing** (MEN-uh-sing) dangerous or causing fear

**penetrated** (PEN-uh-tray-tihd) pierced or passed through

**plaque** (PLAK) a plate with words inscribed on it

**plunged** (PLUHNJD) to bring about quickly and unexpectedly

**rare** (RAIR) very uncommon

**revelation** (rev-uh-LAY-shuhn) the act of making something known

**spirit** (SPIHR-it) a supernatural creature, such as a ghost

**taxidermy** (TAK-suh-dur-mee) stuffing the skins of dead animals and mounting them in lifelike form

## ABOUT THE AUTHOR

Dee Phillips develops and writes nonfiction books for young readers and fiction books—including historical fiction—for middle graders and young adults. She loves to read and write stories that have a twist or an unexpected, thought-provoking ending. Dee lives near the ocean on the southwest coast of England. A keen hiker, her biggest ambition is to one day walk the entire coast of Great Britain.

## ABOUT THE ILLUSTRATOR

Tom Connell has been a professional illustrator since 1987. He works in many styles, but his specialty is realism. Originally painting in gouache and acrylics, he moved on to airbrush and now draws most of his work digitally. He has created artworks for many advertising campaigns, magazines, and several hundred children's books. He lives with his family and two border collies close to the River Kennet in Reading, England.